## Knights of the Ruby Wand

A Magical World Awaits You
Read

THE SECRETS OF DROON

# THE SECRETS OF DROON

— TONY ABBOTT —

## Knights of the Ruby Wand

Illustrated by Royce Fitzgerald
Cover illustration by Tim Jessell

SCHOLASTIC INC.
New York  Toronto  London  Auckland
Sydney  Mexico City  New Delhi  Hong Kong

For my friend Jane Billington
and her remarkable fourth-grade class,
Droonlings all!

For more information about the continuing saga of Droon,
please visit Tony Abbott's website at
www.tonyabbottbooks.com

ISBN: 978-0-545-09886-1

12  11  10  9  8  7  6  5  4  3  2  1        10  11  12  13  14  15/0

Printed in the U.S.A.                                          40
First printing, February 2010

# Contents

# One

# Hunting the Hunters

*Click!*

"And that's why they call me Zabilac," said Neal Kroger as the door of his elementary school swung open. "Genies can open most locks with a simple spell."

"*Break* open most locks, you mean," whispered his friend Julie Rubin, following Neal into the dark school. "This is so wrong."

"Wrong, maybe," said Mrs. Hinkle, mother of their friend Eric, slipping inside behind Julie. "But it's the right thing to do."

"Okay, who brought the flashlight?" Eric's father asked as he quietly shut the door behind them.

The two children and two parents stared at one another in the dim light of the main school hallway.

"Don't look at me," said Neal. "I'm a genie, not a genius."

"Never mind," said Mrs. Hinkle. "A flashlight might give us away. We want to surprise the Hunters. Let's move."

The Hunters were a mysterious trio of Kindu tribesmen — tall and ghostly and evil — who had been sent into the Upper World by the moon dragon, Gethwing, to find something.

Or some*one*.

No one knew exactly what the Hunters

were after. And that was what worried the children.

"Wait," said Mr. Hinkle, pausing to listen. "Do you hear anything?"

Neal shook his head. "It's pretty quiet."

"Are they gone?" asked Mrs. Hinkle.

"Probably not," said Julie. "The Hunters specialize in being quiet. Let's keep going."

As they tiptoed through the dark A-Wing hallway, Julie and Neal sensed that they were not alone in the school.

Since their last adventure, Julie had discovered that she possessed a unique third power. Besides being able to fly and change shape, she could now see visions of events from the past — the long past and the very recent past.

Minutes before, she'd had a vision of the Hunters breaking into her school. If they were still there, she and Neal —

and Eric's parents — would find them, try to discover what they wanted, and stop them.

Stop them? Really?

Neither Julie nor Neal knew if such a thing was even possible. But they had to try. Sending the Hunters to the Upper World was only one part of Gethwing's vast evil plan.

Not long before, Eric had been wounded by a poisoned ice dagger. As he lay ill, the moon dragon cast a spell on him, drawing him out of his wounded state and into the person of Prince Ungast, a powerful boy sorcerer.

Ungast was Eric's evil side and one of the "jewels" in Gethwing's Crown of Wizards. The other jewels were the wicked Princess Neffu and the sorcerer Lord Sparr.

"Maybe Keeah and Max have already

found a cure for Eric's wound," said Mrs. Hinkle as they turned the corner into B-Wing.

"I sure hope so," said Neal. "We need him."

"Droon needs him, too," said Julie.

It certainly did.

Things were getting worse by the hour.

On the heels of Eric's transformation into Ungast, their friend the wizard Galen had been spirited away on a journey by the mysterious genie Anusa.

No one knew if or when he would be back.

"Maybe the Hunters have already gone," said Mr. Hinkle. "It's just so quiet —"

Mrs. Hinkle stopped suddenly.

"Honey?" said Eric's father.

Mrs. Hinkle stared at the fifth locker from the corner. "It's . . . his . . . ," she murmured.

She stepped toward it and reached out, turned the combination lock until it clicked, then pulled open the narrow door. She covered her face with her hands.

"We'll see him soon," said Mr. Hinkle, his hand on her shoulder. "I'm sure of it."

Eric's mother nodded slightly, then removed her son's backpack from the locker. Inside, she found a crumpled lunch bag, a small notebook, and a thermos.

"I'll keep these at home," she said, slinging the backpack over her shoulder.

*Creeeeek* — *thud*. A nearby door closed.

"The gym!" Neal said. "Quietly . . ."

The friends crept down the hall.

Gently opening the gym door, they spotted one of the climbing ropes swinging back and forth, as if someone — or some*thing* — had just brushed against it.

"The Hunters are still here," Julie said.

All at once, three shadowy figures raced across the gym floor toward a door on the far side.

"Cut them off!" shouted Neal. He jumped for the climbing rope and swung all the way across the gym. "Whoa!"

The three figures sprang to one side, and Neal crashed to the floor. "Owww —"

"Here I come!" Mr. Hinkle ran across the bleachers and helped Neal to his feet.

The ghostly figures whizzed past both of them to the far door.

"Oh, no, you don't!" said Julie. She flew across the gym and blocked the door.

One Hunter breathed a command, and all three tore open the sacks they carried over their shoulders. The first unsheathed a short dagger and slashed the air in front of Julie. The second removed a spiked ball and sent it spinning through the air.

"You want to play ball?" said Mrs. Hinkle. "Two can play that game!" She grabbed a bag of basketballs and began hurling them at the Hunter menacing Julie.

"*Vatosh*!" the third Hunter hissed.

The spiked ball whirled at Mrs. Hinkle, narrowly missing her but knocking Eric's backpack from her shoulder and scattering its contents across the floor.

"Hey!" yelled Mr. Hinkle. "That's rude!"

Before Mrs. Hinkle could pick up the backpack, the third Hunter donned a pair of silver boots, took a step, and blurred out of the gym.

He was back in a flash. "*Kethar —*"

With one great leap, all three Hunters sprang to the high windows, where something glinted in the moonlight.

"He's got a bomb!" Neal shouted. "Duck —"

"It's not a bomb," said Mrs. Hinkle. "It's . . . Eric's thermos!"

"What?" said Julie.

A moment later, the three figures had burst through the windows and were outside, dashing across the playground. The woods behind the school swallowed them in an instant. They were gone.

"Why did they steal Eric's thermos?" asked Mrs. Hinkle. "That is just . . . strange."

"I don't know," said Neal. "It was totally empty. I made sure of that a long time ago."

Julie gazed at the place where the Hunters had been. There were watery footprints on the floor. "Guys, the Hunter in the silver boots must have left these. Let's follow them."

Together they tracked the prints from the gym down the hall to the school's swimming pool and stared at the rippling water.

"How very odd," said Mrs. Hinkle.

"And evil," said her husband. "We need to plan our next move."

"And I think we have to go to Droon," said Neal. "Look what just found us."

A black-and-white ball rolled across the wet tiles and stopped at his feet.

"The magic soccer ball followed us here," Neal continued. "Julie, we're needed."

Twenty minutes later, Eric's parents were pacing their kitchen floor and plotting while Neal and Julie hurried down the basement stairs.

"Bad things are piling up," said Julie as they stuffed themselves into the closet under the stairs. "We need Eric and Galen back."

"We'll get them," said Neal. "I mean,

we're an amazing team, right? Wizards, genies, magical powers? We can do anything. As a matter of fact, I've even come up with our own theme song. Want to hear it?"

"Uh . . ."

"*Make way for Zabilac,*" Neal sang softly. "*His turban he will pack. From here to Droon and back. Amazing Zabilac!* Do you like it?"

Julie turned to him. "How is that *our* theme song? It's all about you."

"I'm working on a second verse," said Neal, tugging his big turban over his ears.

Julie sighed. "Keep working."

She turned off the light.

*Whoosh!* The floor of the closet disappeared, and in its place stood the top step of a staircase leading down and away from the basement. The stairs gleamed with all the colors of the rainbow, as if light shone from every step.

"And here we go!" said Neal.

Droon's golden sun peeked over the horizon as the two friends descended the stairs.

"We know this place," said Julie, scanning the landscape below. "I see the plains south of Lumpland. Come on, hurry —"

But no sooner had they reached the bottom step than a giant coil of dust appeared out of nowhere and tore across the ground toward the stairs.

Julie frowned. "That storm looks like it's coming straight for us."

Neal looked over his shoulder. "I'd say we should run back up the stairs, but they're already fading —"

The storm barreled faster toward them.

"Then just plain — run!" cried Julie.

# Two

# In the Dusty, Dusky Morning

"Heeeeelp!" Neal cried as the storm nipped at his heels.

"Don't forget about me," said Julie. "I need help, too!"

Then, just as the swirling coil of dust descended over them —

"Whoa!" cried a voice.

"Whoa — faster!" cried a second voice.

There came a terrible screech and — *poof!* — the storm vanished completely, and a giant spoke-wheeled ship with a big blue sail skidded to a stop inches from the children.

"Hello! Hello!" called two small voices.

Standing on the front deck of the ship, clutching the giant sail's elaborate rigging, were Khan, the pillow-shaped king of the Lumpies, and Batamogi, the fox-eared ruler of the Oobja.

"Children, hop aboard our wind-wagon!" urged Khan. "We're fleeing for our lives!"

"Fleeing what?" asked Julie, climbing up to the deck.

"That!" said Batamogi, pointing across the plains to the distant castle of Zorfendorf. Its walls were surrounded by an army of angry, red-faced Ninn warriors, and circling overhead on the back of a winged black pilka was none other than the evil sorcerer Lord Sparr.

"Oh, no!" Julie gasped.

"Exactly," said Batamogi. "Now, jump downstairs to the main cabin. Keeah's waiting for you. We set sail again!"

"Hoist the hipyank!" called Khan. "Raise the blunderbill! Off we go!"

The ship's sail filled with air, the giant wheels began to roll, and the windwagon shot swiftly across the plains, kicking up a dust storm in its wake.

When Julie and Neal entered the main cabin, they found Princess Keeah, Max the spider troll, and Hob the mask-making imp hovering over a fiery stove top littered with test tubes, pots, and beakers.

Keeah hugged her friends. "I'm so glad you got my message. We need your help."

"Friends, we're doing it!" said Max. "We're finding Eric's cure. Our work is nearly done!"

"No thanks to Lord Sparr!" added Hob, tossing water from a beaker onto a sudden high flame. "The evil one launched a surprise attack on Zorfendorf early this morning. We barely escaped with the fazool —"

"And with our lives!" said Max. "We had to take our laboratory with us in order to finish our work!"

Max and Hob had begun experimenting the moment the tiny drop of fazool had been found. They hoped to discover a cure that would restore Eric to himself.

"Keeah!" Khan called down from the upper deck. "I see the red hills. We must be close!"

Keeah, Julie, and Neal clambered upstairs to the main deck in time to see Batamogi tugging the rigging this way and that. The great sail went slack, and the wagon slowed.

"Why are we stopping?" asked Neal.

"I received a message this morning from Anusa," said Keeah, searching the far plains.

"Anusa?" Julie said. "She took Galen away on his journey. I saw her in my vision."

"Which is why we must meet her," said Keeah. "Hold on . . ."

The princess climbed hand over hand to the top of the main mast that towered over the windwagon. Producing a spyglass, she scanned the brightening sky.

"This is it," she called down. "We're here!"

With a ferocious squeak, the wagon slid to a stop.

To Julie and Neal, there seemed little difference between the spot they were in and any other spot on the grassy plains.

"But how do you know?" asked Neal.

Keeah smiled and pointed directly over-head. A circle of stars was fading quickly from the morning sky. "Anusa's signal."

"Beautiful!" whispered Julie.

"Beautiful, yes," said Max, scrambling on deck with Hob. "But I suspect something is not right. Why is Anusa here, and not with Galen on his genie journey?"

The air around the windwagon twinkled suddenly, and a tall figure dressed in long scarves and veils appeared.

It was the genie Anusa. She wore curly tipped slippers and a jeweled pink turban. She floated through the air and halted a few feet above the wagon.

Neal bowed. "Greetings, Second Genie of the Dove!"

Anusa bowed to everyone, then twice to Neal. "Greetings, Zabilac!"

"Do you have news of our beloved wizard?" asked Max, trembling. "How is his journey going? Well, I hope? Please say yes."

Anusa lowered her lovely hazel eyes. "Alas, it was not I who led your wizard away."

"Not you?" said Keeah.

Julie gasped. "But I saw you in my vision!"

"It was someone else you saw, an imposter," said Anusa, her voice echoing in the cool morning air. "It was *not* Galen's hour to leave you. The beloved wizard was spirited away to a place by someone — and for a reason — I do not know!"

"I should have known!" said Julie. "I remember how worried he looked in my vision. He knew something was wrong."

"This is totally not good," said Neal. "Not only is Eric in trouble and Gethwing attacking Jaffa City and Sparr laying siege

to Zorfendorf and the Hunters messing around upstairs, but Galen's been kidnapped, too?"

"Who would do this?" asked Keeah.

"Who *could* do this?" asked Max.

"Only magic born in the dark days of the long past could trick our wizard so," said Anusa. "Since genies travel in time, I have gone back to Galen's youth and discovered that there exist three objects from his past which — when combined — may help us find him and free him. We need Galen back before Gethwing attacks Jaffa City."

"According to what Eric told me there are only four days before that happens," said Keeah. "What are the objects?"

"Magical, no doubt?" said Khan.

"Magical, indeed," said Anusa. "Long ago, Galen defeated Ko's demons with three weapons.

"The first is a tongue of flame, which bestows knowledge of secret languages. The second is a silver arrow, which can strike anything the shooter desires, either to wound or to heal. The last is the fabled Ruby Wand. The stone in the wand has great power, which renders its possessor nearly invincible. It is this wand that I am asking you to find and bring to me —"

The earth shook, and in the distance a plume of smoke rose over the walls of Zorfendorf.

Hob grumbled. "Time runs short."

"Indeed," said Anusa. "To have any hope of saving Droon, we need Galen back on our front line. The Knights of Silversnow have pledged to find the tongue of flame. I myself will search for the silver arrow. I ask you to find the Ruby Wand."

"We'll do it," said Julie.

"I expected no less," Anusa said with a

smile. "Galen lost the wand ages ago in the wizard wars. But it has recently turned up in a tiny jungle near the shore of Doobesh."

"We'll take the windwagon as far as the cliffs south of Agrah-Voor," said Keeah, "then continue on foot from there. Max?"

"Good plan," said the spider troll. "We will keep up our work and hope for success —"

"And, remember, no more stove-top fires!" said Hob.

"Beware of Gethwing's armies," said Anusa. "If Galen's enemies learn of the wand, they will stop at nothing to possess it. Friends, go!"

# Three

# Beasts, Beasts Everywhere

And go they did.

As the genie Anusa faded into the sparkling morning air, Keeah's windwagon bounced its way swiftly toward the southern coast.

Soon the friends spotted black smoke coiling from the Panjibarrh caves to the east. All up and down the dusty hills, they spied the glinting blades of Ninn warriors.

"My poor homeland," said Batamogi. "Invaded. Spoiled. Someday we will return."

"Gethwing is destroying Droon," said Neal. "I can't wait until we're back together again. Eric. Galen. Everyone. We'll stop that creep."

As they often had before, Keeah found her thoughts turning to Eric. She imagined her dear friend in thrall to the moon dragon, in the guise of Ungast but lingering as himself deep inside.

She knew that Eric was still there, because she had spoken to him. But time was running out. For him. For Galen. For Droon.

"Look there," said Batamogi. "Something is flying toward us from the west."

A twinkle of light zigzagged across the blue sky. As swiftly as a bird in flight, it coiled all the way down the main mast and circled Keeah, sprinkling beads of light in her hair.

"Flink!" gasped Keeah. "Please show yourself!"

Flink was Galen's messenger, a rare and friendly sprite who flew at the speed of light. With a shake of her tiny wings, she settled on Keeah's shoulder. There was a kind of song to Flink's words. Keeah listened closely, then nodded.

"Really? They are?" she said. "But where?"

More gentle singing filled the air.

"What is it?" asked Julie.

"My parents are nearby," said the princess. "They have news. Flink, lead the way. Khan, Batamogi, set a course for Rivertangle!"

The light gleamed brightly and flitted off.

Under Batamogi and Khan's skilled

direction, the windwagon followed at top speed, racing over the plains until the deep whacking of drums made them slow down.

"I smell danger!" said Khan, his nose lifted into the air. "Mogi, pull behind that ridge."

"Aye-aye, cocaptain," said the Oobja king.

When the wagon stopped, the children scrambled up the rigging to the lookout post. At first, all they saw were clouds of brown dust moving across a distant plain.

"More windwagons?" said Neal.

"I don't think so," said Julie. "Oh —"

A black tower moved slowly out of the dusty clouds and glinted in the morning sun. Then another appeared. And another.

"What are those things?" asked Neal.

"Battle towers!" hissed Batamogi, his tall ears shaking. "Seven, eight, ten of them!"

"So far," said Keeah.

They spied a legion of fierce-looking lion-headed beasts dragging the towers across the earth.

On the summit of each tower stood an armed wingwolf barking orders to the battalions of lion beasts below. "Faster! Faster!"

Keeah looked from the towers to the sky, then over her shoulder.

"They're making their way to Jaffa City," she said. She felt her head begin to pound. An image of her home city came into her mind. It was shining pink in the bold sunshine, like a thing newborn. She recalled her little room.

But the thundering earth, the creaking of burdened wheels, the calling of the wingwolves, and the grunting of the lions dissolved the momentary scene, and she found her eyes welling with tears.

"We'll stop them," said Neal.

"Hob will do all he can," said the imp.

"We all will!" promised Khan.

Keeah wiped her eyes. "We will," she said. "But not right now. The towers won't arrive at Jaffa City for another day, perhaps two. Let's hope we have Galen back before then. And Eric, too. Sail on. Sail on!"

And so they sailed on, following Flink's glittering light, riding the wind across the open plains until they arrived at the bank of a wide river leading into the vast blue Sea of Droon. Bobbing near the riverbank stood the seagoing vessel known as the *Jaffa Wind*.

Keeah's parents, King Zello and Queen Relna, paced the ship's deck, attended by a dozen royal soldiers.

As soon as the wagon rolled to a

stop, Keeah and her friends jumped on board the ship. Wasting no time, they told of the battle towers and what Anusa had said to them.

Zello breathed deeply, grasped the handle of his great club, but did not unsheathe it.

"Anusa appeared to us as well," he said. "I might forbid you to go to Doobesh were it not for Galen. We need him now."

"You will never guess what new enemy is coming to join Gethwing," said Queen Relna.

"Uh-oh," said Neal. "Who?"

"Only the worst, most despicable, and most fearful creatures!" said Zello.

"Father, who?" asked Keeah.

Zello gritted his teeth and pulled out his club. "The Warriors of the Skorth!"

A shudder of fear went through the friends.

The Warriors of the Skorth were ferocious skeleton creatures who were neither dead nor alive. They were beings from the most ancient days of the evil empire of Goll, conjured back from the dead by Lord Sparr. They had roamed Droon ever since.

"I totally remember the moment Sparr brought those bad dudes out of retirement," said Neal. "I really don't like them."

"Who does?" said Batamogi.

"Maybe their mothers?" said Neal. "If they even *have* mothers. Which I doubt."

"The Skorth navy, some twenty ships at last count, is even now leaving the dark coasts of Mintar," Zello said. "Once they pass through the dreaded Horns of Ko, they will be in the Sea of Droon, with nothing to stop them from joining the siege of Jaffa City."

"Alas, our navy is scattered," said Relna. "The *Jaffa Wind* is our only vessel. We've sent for help, but the nearest ship is hours away."

Keeah recalled how the Skorth had summoned their navy from the depths of the sea. It was a fleet of haunted ghost ships with torn rigging and battered hulls.

"We need our friends with us," she said. "One by one, we must bring them back. Eric with his cure, Galen with his three weapons. Friends, we have to get that wand before anyone else does."

"We're with you," said Neal.

Zello turned to his daughter. "Let us meet tomorrow on the Saladian Plains."

"In the meantime," said Relna, "we sail with but our single ship to keep the Skorth from our doors. Now, go. Fly like the wind. Our time will soon run out!"

So with Khan and Batamogi as drivers and Keeah, Julie, and Neal high atop the lookout, the windwagon continued on its way. Below the deck, Max and Hob kept up their bubbly experiments.

It was nearly noon when they arrived at the cliffs near the northern coast of Doobesh.

"Stay here and keep working," Keeah told Hob, Max, and Batamogi. "Julie, Neal, and I will scale down the cliffs to the jungle below. Signal us with a flare if you spy any danger. I'll conjure an invisibility fog around the wagon so no one will see you."

"Thank you," said Max, bowing to the princess. "May luck be with us all."

After watching the windwagon vanish in magical fog, the three children trekked to the crest of the cliffs.

Keeah pulled out her spyglass. "Doobesh is a strange country," she said. "Lawless in places. We must be very —"

*Thoom! Thoom!*

The friends turned. To the east stood a

set of massive rocks, seventy feet tall, carved in the image of Emperor Ko's bull-shaped head. They separated the dismal Serpent Sea from the sparkling blue waters of the Sea of Droon.

"The Horns of Ko," whispered Julie.

As the children watched—*thoooom!*—the giant rocks thundered shut.

When the Horns of Ko crashed together, they shattered any enemy ship that tried to sail between them, thus protecting the Dark Lands from an invasion by sea but allowing enemy ships to enter the Sea of Droon at will.

Keeah gasped. "Look . . ."

Rising up beyond the horizon were one . . . two . . . three tall masts. Ragged black cloth fluttered from the yardarms. Garlands of seaweed clung to the tattered rigging.

"The Skorth are coming!" said Neal.

On the tip of each mast was a blood-red flag emblazoned with a pattern of four jagged dragon wings arched high.

Keeah trembled. "Gethwing's banner."

Even from that distance, the kids could see that the ghostly ship's black hull was cracked and full of holes, yet it sailed magically — and swiftly — over the waves toward the Horns.

"We should call Flink to warn your parents," said Julie.

But before they could, a series of peculiar sounds coiled up from the rocks below.

*Cling! Plong! Blunk! Pling!*

Keeah looked at her friends, then spoke silently to them.

**Someone's coming up the path. Hide!**

# Four

## Sisters, Sisters

*Thunk! Pling!*

As the odd sounds grew louder, the children scrambled to hide among the rocks, but found a place big enough for only two, and Julie and Keeah got there first.

***Thanks a bunch!*** Neal scowled silently. Crouching in plain sight, he pulled his turban completely over himself and muttered a spell.

As the turban took on the appearance of a large stone, an old woman dressed in rags strolled slowly up the winding path toward the kids' hiding place. Her skin was the color of a pistachio, and her nose was so long it nearly touched the tip of her chin.

"A witch?" whispered Julie.

Keeah nodded. "Without a doubt. Look."

A stringed instrument similar to a harp hovered in the air next to the woman, and whenever she murmured, the harp sang out as if in answer to her.

"Are you certain?" said the witch. "And it turned up right here in Doobesh? When?"

*Plang-a-ling-lang-plonk-plonk-diddle-ding!*

"Last week?" said the woman. "Hmmm. And you say a little weasel found it?"

*Lang!* went the harp.

"Fine, but is the magic gem still in it?"

*Bloink!*

The woman broke into a laugh. "Excellent! Our long journey is over. We must tell my sister! Come along!" The woman hurried up the path but stopped suddenly.

"What's this, then?" she said. "A new rock? Right in the middle of the path?" She stared at it for a moment, then gave it a swift kick.

Neal pretended not to feel it, but Keeah saw his face twist in pain beneath the turban.

"I don't recall this rock," said the woman. "I think it should go away. . . . Hebba-zebba!"

At once, the "rock" lifted into the air.

"Don't throw me!" cried Neal.

"Aha!" snapped the woman. "An imposter! Show yourself at once!"

Neal jumped to the ground and became himself. "Please don't put a spell on me —"

"Indeed!" The old woman scratched her long nose and pointed a skinny finger at him. "Wait a moment! I know you!"

"You do?" said Neal.

The woman blinked. "Nope. Not a clue."

"My name is Neal," he told her.

"Don't tell me!" said the old woman, closing her eyes and pressing her fingers to her temples. "I'm getting it. You're . . . Neal!"

He frowned. "But I just told you that."

"You told me because I entered your mind and *forced* you to tell me," she said. "That's the kind of power I have!"

Now it was Neal's turn to blink. "Wow. That *is* powerful."

Julie and Keeah popped out of their hiding place, and the harp went *blong!*

"Oh, I really *do* know you!" said the witch, bowing to Keeah. "You are the Princess of Droon!"

"I am," said Keeah. "And we couldn't help hearing you and your harp. Do you know something about the Ruby Wand?"

The old woman narrowed her eyes first at Keeah, then at Julie and Neal. "I do. My name is Magdy, and I've just heard that the wand has turned up nearby. My sister and I have been searching for it for a long time."

"Oh, really?" said Julie. "Why?"

"Because, long ago, we made it!"

"You did?" said Neal. "For Galen?"

Magdy swooned. "Galen! Lovely boy!"

"He's no longer a boy," said Julie. "He's been kidnapped. We've been sent by a genie to find the wand. It can help free him."

The harp floated very near Magdy and plinked gently in her ear. The old woman's thin lips lifted into a smile.

"Quite right," she said. "You must meet my twin sister, Hagdy. Come into our parlor!"

The old woman hustled the kids up the path to her "parlor," which was no more than a damp little cave overlooking Doobesh.

Before entering, Keeah glanced once more at the distant Serpent Sea. Two more black-sailed ships had appeared on the horizon.

"Father and Mother," she sighed. "The battle is coming."

A small fire lit the insides of the cave, and next to the fire sat an old woman who was the spitting image of Magdy.

"Hagdy, I bring strangers," said Magdy.

"Greetings!" said Hagdy.

"Greetings —" Keeah began.

"Hush!" cried Hagdy. "I hear a voice!"

Everyone froze.

"Never mind. It stopped," said Hagdy. "So . . . greetings, again!"

"Greetings —" said Keeah.

"Hush! I hear it again!" said Hagdy.

"You hear it because it's Princess Keeah trying to speak to you," explained Magdy.

"Oh," said Hagdy. "Hello, dear."

Magdy leaned toward the children. "Please forgive my sister. She is . . . well . . . old."

"But you're twins," said Neal.

"I'm younger by a whole minute!" said Magdy. "Sister! These nice children have come because of the wand. They . . . want it."

Hagdy raised her eyes from the fire and gave her sister a private look. "They do, do they? But why do you want the Ruby Wand?"

"We need it to help Galen," said Neal.

"Ooh, Galen!" said Hagdy. "Such a handsome young fellow he was! Clean-shaven. Cute cheeks. Just right for pinching!"

"He liked me best," said Magdy.

"But I saw him first!" said Hagdy.

Magdy grumbled. "You see everything first. You're older, don't forget."

Peeking out the cave entrance, Keeah saw more dark sails edging over the horizon. That made five Skorth ghost ships so far.

"We need to move this along," she said. "Can you tell us what the wand does?"

The two sisters exchanged another look and shared a tiny smile.

"That depends whether you're a good person or not," said Magdy. "Our harp tells us a weasel named Anga has the wand now —"

*Thunggggg!* went the harp.

"That is, *Duke* Anga," said Hagdy. "He was a common tree weasel until he found our wand. Now he fancies himself a duke!"

"We can show you the best way to Anga's amazing palace," said Magdy.

"It's treacherous otherwise," added Hagdy.

"Just a moment," said Julie. She pulled Neal and Keeah out of earshot of the two sisters and lowered her voice. "We could use their help, but what about the looks they've been giving each other?"

"I saw," said Keeah. "Can we trust them?"

"Galen trusted them to make a wand

for him," said Neal. "But if it was before he had a beard, that was a very long time ago."

They realized that Galen *had* trusted the twins, even if it was long before. And if the wand was as powerful as Anusa said, they might need the sisters' help to get it back.

Keeah nodded. "I guess we don't have much choice, do we? Or much time."

"Right," said Julie. "Let's risk it."

Keeah turned to the twin sisters. "Please take us to Duke Anga," she said.

"Absolutely!" said Magdy, stepping outside and looking up the path. "You need us."

"We're excellent guides," said Hagdy, looking past her sister down the path.

"Good," said Keeah. "Lead on."

"This way!" the sisters announced together.

And they walked off in opposite directions.

# Five

## Ambush in the Bushes

"Stop!" said Julie.

The two sisters froze in their tracks, turned, and stared at each other.

"Silly me!" said Magdy. "Of course, you're right. It's completely that way —"

"No, sister, you're right," said Hagdy. "It's that way —"

They walked off in opposite directions again.

"Stop again!" said Keeah. She pointed

to a middle path that led straight down the cliff to the jungle. "I'm going this way."

"That seems fine," said Magdy.

"We'll follow you," said Hagdy.

"Because you need us," said Magdy.

The children wondered if they needed the witch sisters at all, but they descended the cliff anyway. Hagdy and Magdy followed, cackling to each other, while the floating harp trailed behind them, plinking softly to itself.

The jungle of Doobesh stretched for miles from the cliffs to the Sea of Droon. Its trees formed a lush green world that was home to thousands of birds winging their way from branch to branch.

When the little group finally reached the foot of the cliff, Keeah could no longer see the Skorth ships, but she knew more of them were closing in at every moment.

"We have to be quick," she said. "Get in, find Anga, get the wand, get out."

Magdy nudged her sister, who suddenly went still. They nodded in unison, and the harp jumped. *BLANG!*

"Poof!" said Hagdy.

"Puff!" said Magdy.

Before the children knew what was happening, the twin sisters and their harp vanished in a cloud of smoke, and the jungle came alive with hundreds of shapes.

"Surround the attackers!" cried a voice.

"Tree weasels!" hissed Neal. "The sisters betrayed us. Run!"

Too late.

Hundreds of small figures, furry from the tips of their noses to the tips of their tails, swung down from the branches and surrounded the children.

The creatures had big cheeks and

short, pointed ears and wore puffy green trousers and matching vests. They thrashed stubby, narrow sticks about menacingly.

"Stand back!" said Julie. "We'll fight!"

"Silence!" snarled one of the weasels, who was a bit taller than the others. He swaggered up to the kids, then narrowed his eyes at Keeah's crown.

"I am Pinch," he said. "And you are . . ."

"Princess Keeah," said Keeah.

"You didn't let me finish!" Pinch growled. "I'll start again. I am Pinch. And you are . . . captured! We will take you to Duke Anga!"

Neal nudged his friends. *Should we fight?*

Keeah's mind leaped from thought to thought. Maybe the witch sisters *had* betrayed them. Maybe this *was* a trap. But they still needed Anga's wand, and the weasels would bring them to Anga.

*No. Let's become their prisoners. For now,* Keeah said.

*For now,* said Julie with a slight nod.

*But not for long, right?* asked Neal.

*I hope not,* said Keeah. *Don't use your powers. Let's play along.*

"Pinch, take us to your leader," she said.

"Oh, I will," said Pinch, scruffing the furry tuft on his head. "But you won't enjoy it. Boys, a little marching music, please?"

On cue, the weasels began to hum. *"Pah-rum! Pah-rum! Pah-rum-pum-pum!"*

"Have you noticed that there's a lot of music on this adventure?" whispered Julie.

"Maybe before it's over, I'll get to sing my theme song again," said Neal.

Julie frowned. "Let's hope it doesn't come to that."

The weasels hummed along the winding jungle paths to the foot of a structure more like an enormous tree house than a palace. The building had many levels and was made entirely of branches and leaves, trees and vines, and stairs, walkways, ladders, and bridges that connected each level to the next.

The palace was a living structure, blossoming with magnificent flowers from the jungle floor all the way up to a tower nearly touching the high jungle canopy.

"*Pah — rum-pum-pummmm!*" the weasels hummed, then stopped.

Silence fell over the jungle.

No one moved.

Keeah felt the seconds tick by. In her mind's eye, she saw more and more Skorth ships approaching the shore, their ghostly sails billowing in the wind. She wished she already had the wand and could return to help her parents stop the Skorth, and hasten Eric's and Galen's return.

Still the seconds ticked by.

And still nothing happened.

"Now what?" Neal asked.

Pinch made a face. "Wait for it . . ."

Then, with a loud squeak and a soft snapping of branches, something descended through the leaves from high overhead. It was a sort of cradle, like a hammock, wide from end to end and suspended by vines from the tower's summit.

Sitting on the cradle, like a child on a swing, was a weasel whose head was slightly larger than the others'.

And while Pinch and the others wore puffy pants and vests, this creature wore a long blue coat decorated with gold chains, medals, and buttons. Bright golden fringes dangled from each padded shoulder.

A tall tuft of silvery fur grew straight up from the center of his head.

"Ahem . . . ," he said, looking at Pinch.

"Ahem?" Pinch repeated. Then he blinked. "Oh. Right! All . . . hail . . . Duke . . . Anga!"

There was a soft grumble among the weasel troops, but eventually they repeated Pinch's words. "All hail Duke Anga. . . ."

"Quite right," said the duke.

When he hopped down from the cradle to the jungle floor and strode on his hind legs, the children saw that Anga was two feet tall from tail to tuft but had the puffed-up demeanor of a weasel twice that size.

He stopped in front of the kids and scowled. "In-*vaders*! Attacking Anga's palace, are you?"

"Not really —" Keeah started.

"On your *knees*!" the weasel ruler shouted. "So I can look you *in the eyes*!"

"Duke Anga commands you to obey!" said Pinch. Then he whispered, "Believe me, you'd better. He gets kind of upset. . . ."

"We really do mean you no harm," said Keeah, kneeling with her friends.

"Ha! And *ha*!" Anga said, pushing his little button of a nose into Keeah's face. "And again, I proclaim, *HA*!"

He suddenly stopped talking and stared at Neal's turban. "What's that on your head?"

"It's a —"

"Did I tell you to *speak*?" screamed Anga.

"Well, actually, you did —"

"It *looks* like some sort of big *muffin*!" said Anga, poking Neal's turban.

Neal said nothing. His eyes glazed over, and his friends knew he was thinking about muffins.

Suddenly, Anga gasped. "Hold on! Strangers in my jungle? I wonder if you are the ones foretold by the mysterious prophecy!"

"What prophecy?" asked Julie.

"Silence!" shouted Duke Anga. "I will tell you what prophecy!"

Hanging on Anga's waist was a sheath. Slowly, he drew from the sheath not a sword but a shaft of gleaming brass. A giant red stone — a ruby — was fixed near its tip. The ruby glowed brightly, shedding a warm crimson light over all of them.

*The Ruby Wand!* said Keeah.

The moment he held the wand, Anga seemed to swell a few sizes larger. "This here wand has magic all over it, and I have waited my whole life for its prophecy to come true!"

"But, Duke Anga, you didn't find the wand until last Saturday," said Pinch.

"*Duke* Anga?" the weasel ruler said, narrowing his eyes. "You remind me that I've been considering a promotion. From now on, call me . . . *Prince* Anga!" He paused. "I'm *waiting*. . . ."

"All hail *Prince* Anga," chorused the weasels.

"Very good," said their leader. "Now, according to the prophecy, the owner of the wand commands the fabled Knights of the Ruby Wand. Perhaps you children are them."

"But maybe the prophecy's come true already," said Pinch. "Did you ever think of that? I mean, maybe *me* and the *other* weasels are the Knights of the Ruby Wand —"

"Oh, don't make me laugh!" snarled Anga. "You? You are hardly *knights* at all! Not to mention knights of any *wand*. Not to mention a *ruby* wand. Look at you. You are not the least . . . *knight*like."

Pinch and his men took deep breaths and stepped back. "Yes, Prince Anga."

"What did you call me?" said Anga. "I am no longer *Prince*. I am — are you ready?"

"Are we ever?" asked Pinch.

"*King* Anga!" said the weasel ruler. "Yes, that's better. As my first kingly act, I demand that these *children* submit to the *trial*!"

"What trial?" said Julie.

Anga grinned, and his teeth gleamed. "The trial that proves if you are *worthy* to be my *knights* of the Ruby Wand or not. If you are *not* worthy, I will know you are *attackers*! And if you are attackers, I shall be . . . angry!"

As Anga finished speaking, the ruby flared. The little weasel's eyes changed from green to red. The tuft of fur on his head turned spiky. Inch by inch, he grew taller than the children. His teeth curved into sharp fangs.

When he clutched the wand's handle and pointed it at the children, large black clouds raced across the sky overhead. The wind rushed and howled among the trees.

"Holy cow, what's happening?" said Julie.

"The *trial*!" Anga shouted, his voice deep as thunder. "Force them to enter . . . the patio!"

"That doesn't sound so bad," Neal muttered.

"I didn't finish!" Anga snapped. "The Patio . . . OF TERROR! Only if you make it all the way to my tower will you be my knights. Pinch, to the patio with them. And be rough!"

"As you say, Sire," said Pinch.

As roughly as he possibly could — which fortunately was not all that rough — Pinch led the children off to the Patio . . .

. . . OF TERROR!

# Six

# The Terrifying Patio!

With a cold laugh, King Anga hopped into his cradle and was hoisted all the way up to his palace-top throne room.

"Move along now," Pinch said to the children, prodding them with his stick. He marched the kids around the back of the palace. "Prince Anga is already miffed. You don't want him any madder."

"*King* Anga," said Julie. "You said '*Prince*.'"

"Right. Well, it keeps changing, doesn't it?" Pinch said as they neared the patio. "It's probably changing again while we're doing this. Don't know how much higher he can go, though. King's about the top as far as titles go."

*We have to end this silly business and get that wand,* Neal said silently.

*But how?* asked Julie.

*I'm working on it,* said Keeah.

At least, she was trying to.

But her mind was a jumble of worries. There were the wand's strange control of nature, the fact that Anga wouldn't give it up, the approach of the Skorth navy, and her parents' safety. To say nothing of Eric's curse — poor Eric! — the battle towers, Galen's kidnapping, and the five days before the attack that were now four and would soon be three.

It was all so . . . overwhelming!

"Here you are, then!"

The weasel captain halted in front of a gate that led into the back of Anga's palace. Towering over the gate was the giant construction itself, made of tree limbs and planks that rose hundreds of feet in the air, all the way to the tip of the tower, where Anga now sat.

"Into the patio," said Pinch. "Maybe you'll find Anga at the top. Maybe not. See you . . . Well, no, we probably *won't* see you."

"Hold on," said Julie. "*This* is the patio?"

"Sorry, yes," said Pinch. "Many poor souls have been lost in it. Sad, really."

"It doesn't look like any patio I've ever seen," said Neal. "And I *have* a patio."

Pinch sighed. "Well, it *started* as a normal patio off the back of the palace. I mean, Anga always wanted one —"

"King Anga," said Julie.

"Yeah, him," said Pinch. "But since he found the wand, he got these big ideas. He told us to add stairs and another level, then a slide back to the first level. But we made the slide too long, so we had to build a third level to slide down from. But that turned out to be too tall, so we needed more stairs, but they were too short. So we added a ladder, but Anga said, 'Put a curve in it,' which meant adding a level between two and three. But when we renumbered the levels, we somehow got level five, which was just sitting there with no way to get to it, so we added a bridge, which runs all the way up to the balcony on level seven —"

"Level seven?" said Neal. "What happened to level six?"

"Six is Anga's unlucky number," said Pinch. "So there is no sixth level. Which makes it even more confusing. So Anga decided to turn the patio into a trial for finding his knights. And here we are!"

"What's taking so long?" Anga shouted down from his perch.

"Teaching a history lesson!" Pinch called.

"Make *them* history!" called Anga. "Now!"

Anga's eyes turned red, and the sky began to darken once more. Lightning flashed.

"Sorry," Pinch said to the children. "It's my job."

The weasel troops armed themselves with bows and arrows and stood guard at the patio entrance to prevent the kids from escaping.

The children had no choice but to enter.

The Patio of Terror was as terrifying as it appeared. With every step the kids took, they seemed to get deeper into the structure and farther away from any way out. Here, the planks sank beneath their feet. There, a bamboo wall flipped and sent them into a blind alley. The ladder upward only took them down again, and they had to start all over.

"This is like my brain in math class," said Neal. "Should we just fly out of here?"

"I don't like the look of those arrows," said Julie. "Pinch and his men are probably just as afraid of Anga as we are. They might fire."

"And we probably couldn't find our way out if we tried," said Keeah. "I think I'm in math class with you, Neal."

They pressed on. The higher they went, the more Anga scowled at them and the worse the weather became.

Black clouds swirled over the jungle treetops, and sharp winds battered the

wooden framework of the patio. When they reached the third level, Anga howled, and lightning bolts sizzled at them from the Ruby Wand.

"This is so crazy!" said Neal, ducking under a wobbly balcony. "He has to be stopped!"

When they made it to the fifth level, Keeah's breath caught in her throat. Peeking through the vines, she could see the first Skorth ship sail safely beyond the Horns of Ko. Two more ships were close behind.

In the distance she saw a royal vessel steam toward the *Jaffa Wind*, but even two ships were no match for the gathering Skorth navy.

"Maybe we should split up," Keeah said.

"Less chatting and more terror down there!" shouted Anga. "I'm watching you!"

As his anger grew, so did the strength of the lightning bolts exploding overhead.

"We have to do something," said Julie, ducking away from an assault of frozen rain.

Neal peered up at the tower's top, then back down to the entrance. "I figure only one of us can escape, and that's you, Keeah."

"Me?" she said. "Why me?"

"Because Julie and I can change shape, and you can't. The two of us can pretend to be Neal and Julie or Julie and Keeah or Keeah and Neal, so they won't miss you. But you and me or you and Julie can only pretend to be either Keeah and Julie or Keeah and Neal, but not Neal and Julie or Julie and Keeah or Keeah and Neal. See the problem?"

Keeah stared into his eyes. "Up close, actually."

"You're welcome," said Neal.

Lightning crashed inches away.

"I — said — more — terror!" cried Anga.

Wasting no time, Julie twisted her heels and suddenly looked like Keeah while Neal muttered a word and instantly looked like Julie.

"I still have that headache," Keeah said. "But good luck."

"We'll pretty much need it," said Julie.

"I know you will," said the princess.

While icy rain battered the patio stairs, Keeah jumped down a slide, ducked under a wobbly platform, darted around one corner after another, hurried across little bridges, clambered up short stairs, and jumped down long ones. Soon she saw Pinch and his men guarding the entrance. In her head, she knew they were as much victims of Anga's wrath as she and her friends were.

"I won't hurt them," she promised herself.

Doubling back, she found an odd angle in one level. Waiting for the next lightning blast, she flicked her fingers. The moment the sky exploded, she blasted her way out of the patio and darted into the thick jungle.

Hunching her shoulders low, she kept running. As she raced away, she tried to form a plan. But there were so many things to consider. Pinch. The witch sisters. Anga's bizarre power over nature. Her captured friends. And the Warriors of the Skorth!

"It's too much," she said.

Glancing overhead, she knew that behind Anga's storm, the sun must be waning. The day was already more than half over. "Time is passing!"

Keeah used all her strength to push her way through the dense, dangling vines. She could see the edge of the jungle. Only a few more feet and she would be out.

And then — "Oh, no!"

When she saw the shore, she froze in her tracks. Seven Skorth ships already sailed north on the Sea of Droon, heading directly for her parents' ship.

"How can I stop them? What can I do —"

"You can be captured!" cried a familiar voice. All at once — *whooomp!* — a thick web of vines fell over Keeah, and she was caught.

"Take her away, boys!" cried Pinch.

## Seven

# Keeah's Plan of Plans!

The weasel troops marched Keeah away but stopped when one of Pinch's fellow guards gasped. "Sir, look!"

They all turned to see a blur of dragon wings streaking the afternoon sky.

"Gethwing!" murmured Keeah.

And there, on the dragon's back, sat none other than the purple-cloaked figure of Prince Ungast, his hand thrust toward the east.

Keeah shuddered, guessing that Gethwing and Ungast were on their way to inspect the battle towers the kids had seen earlier.

*Eric . . . I . . . we need you! What would you do in my place?*

But her cursed friend and the moon dragon soared over the hills and were soon gone.

*THOOM!* The earth quaked with the sound of the Horns of Ko thundering shut behind the last Skorth vessel. All twenty ships were now sailing swiftly on the open sea.

Keeah knew they would soon spot the *Jaffa Wind* and launch an attack her parents would surely lose.

"They'll be at Jaffa City in two days at most," said Pinch's comrade.

"Ah, Jaffa City. Spent a lovely week there once," said Pinch. "Too bad those odd bonehead men will probably tear the place down. Sad."

Keeah knew that Eric might revolt against Gethwing now, fight the moon dragon. But in doing so, he would lose the big battle. He was doing everything he could to hold on, to find a way to defeat Gethwing from the inside once and for all.

She felt the same way. She was angry. She wanted to blast everything in sight. She wanted to steal the wand and fight the Skorth and get it all done. But being angry wouldn't solve her problems. It only clouded her thinking. It wasn't helping. So she imagined Eric's face in front of her, speaking to her.

She imagined what he would say.

And then she knew.

Like Eric, she had to make sure all the parts of her plan came together at the same time. She would have to do everything at once — which meant that her plan would have to be big. Bigger than big. There would be lots of phases to it. If it was going to work, everyone had to play a part.

Her friends. Pinch. The weasels. The weird sisters. Anga. Even the terrifying Skorth Warriors.

Everyone.

"I have it!" she said.

Pinch jumped. "You have something? Anga probably wants it. You should turn it over."

Keeah knew she was taking a big chance, but there was something in Pinch's brown eyes that told her the weasels had been happier before regular old Anga became King Anga.

"Things haven't been right since he found the wand, have they?" she asked.

Pinch scratched his chin. "Well, for

one thing, the weather was a lot better back then."

"I think we can change that," said Keeah. "But . . . I'll need your help."

"Our help? We're enemies!" said Pinch.

Keeah looked at him. "Are we really? Do I look like your enemy? I think we're both enemies of that terrible moon dragon."

"I don't like him; that's true," said Pinch.

"I know you're not happy with Anga," Keeah said. "Let's teach him a little lesson."

"Us? Teach *him* a lesson?" said Pinch. "That would be different."

"And dangerous," said another weasel.

"But maybe fun?" said a third.

Pinch turned to the other weasels. They mumbled amongst themselves for a few moments. Then the captain turned back to Keeah and smiled. "Fine, but only if you promise not to hurt Anga."

Keeah breathed a sigh of relief. She didn't want to fight the cute little tree weasels.

"Here's what I'm thinking," she said. "King Anga is waiting for the Knights of the Ruby Wand, right? We have to convince Anga that the *Skorth* are the Knights of the Ruby Wand."

"*Those* Skorth?" asked Pinch, looking nervously at the ghostly ships. "You'll need lots of luck getting Anga to agree to that!"

"No," said Keeah. "*You'll* need lots of luck. Because you're going to tell him."

"Me?" said Pinch.

"You," said Keeah.

"Why will the Skorth stop here?" he asked.

"Leave that to me," said Keeah.

Closing her eyes, she murmured a dozen mysterious words, and a ball of dazzling light appeared, buzzing over her head.

"She's very sparkly," said Pinch.

"Flink, I have a mission for you!" Keeah said. As she spoke to the sprite, Flink responded in words that sounded like the tinkle of tiny bells. The next moment, the sprite grew twisty little horns. Her beautiful wings turned ragged. Stingers coiled out from her tail.

"That's one ugly bug, that is," said Pinch.

"The better to convince the ugly Skorth," said Keeah. "Flink, I want you to pretend to be a bug sent from Gethwing. Tell Nok, the Skorth commander, that King Anga awaits his arrival. Tell him that Anga has kept Gethwing's Ruby Wand safe just for him."

"Wait, that's not true," said Pinch. "Is it?"

"No," said Keeah. "Gethwing may not even know about the Wand. But the Skorth won't know that. Flink, you'll know the Skorth leader by his helmet of silver bones. Tell him to come with two others."

Keeah hadn't quite worked out the later phases of her plan, but she knew that more than a few Skorth would be a problem, not just for Anga, but for her and her friends as well.

"But . . . won't they hurt King Anga?" asked Pinch. "I mean, he can be a little . . . you know . . . but he's our . . . you know . . ."

"I'll make sure the Skorth don't hurt Anga," said Keeah. "They won't hurt my friends, either, especially after we're all together again."

Pinch frowned. "But your friends are trapped in the . . . Oh, I get it. You want us to *free* your friends from the Patio . . . of Terror!"

"You are a noble Pinch, Pinch," said Keeah.

"But you don't want the Skorth to have the wand, either, do you?" the weasel asked.

"No, I don't," said Keeah, scanning the nearest path to the top of the cliffs. "But we do want to delay them until the royal navy arrives. According to my plan, when the Skorth come here, we'll take the wand from Anga."

"Oh! You have a *plan*!" said Pinch.

"Well, most of one," said Keeah. "This is Phase One, but believe me, it's just the tip of the iceberg."

"There are icebergs?" asked Pinch.

Keeah took a deep breath. "What I mean is, can't you just imagine what will happen when the Skorth demand Anga give them his wand?"

Pinch snorted a laugh. "Oh, yes! When you put it that way, it's a wonderful plan! Exquisite trickery! Such cleverness. Absolutely —"

"Uh, I don't see it," said another weasel.

"Right. Me, either," said Pinch. "Explain it again, please?"

# Eight

## All Those Phases!

But there was barely time to explain it once, for the Skorth navy was already moving away from the Doobesh coast and on to open sea.

As Flink swept into the air, and Keeah and the weasels hurried inland, the princess knew exactly what she needed to do, where she needed to be, and the moment she needed to be there.

Mostly.

Keeah mostly knew those things.

But there wasn't time to figure out all the fine points. Time was running out.

The instant they arrived among the trees just beyond Anga's patio, Keeah stopped.

"Here's where I must leave you," she said.

"We'll do our part," said the weasel leader. "Troops, follow me to free the boy and girl!"

The weasels disappeared into the green thickness of the jungle, leaving Keeah alone with her thoughts.

"Phase One, Flink. Phase Two, Pinch to free Neal and Julie. Phase Four, convince Anga that the Skorth are the knights. And now . . . Phase Three!"

Not at all certain that her plan would work but knowing she had no time to lose, Keeah ran to the base of the cliff. She climbed up the steepest — and shortest — path to the top and found the cave of the witch sisters.

"Here goes. . . ."

She boldly stepped into the cave, making sure her fingers sizzled with violet sparks.

"You sisters betrayed us!" she said, pretending to be angry.

"Oh!" said Magdy in surprise. "Don't hurt us! We're really very good witches!"

"We wanted the wand because we're old and have lost most of our magic!" said Hagdy.

"Your sparks look dangerous," said Magdy.

"They can be," said Keeah. "But I promise no one will get hurt as long as you . . . make me something."

The twin sisters blinked.

"Make?"

"Something?"

"Really?"

"We'll do it!"

In a flash, Hagdy and Magdy dragged a workbench from the depths of the cave. While they dusted off their old magical equipment — bottles and bowls, books and scrolls — Keeah described exactly what she wanted.

"A magic wand, identical to the Ruby Wand in every way, but instead of being destructive, I want it to do something different."

"Something happy?" asked Magdy. "Like make balloons?"

"Or blossom with flowers?" added Hagdy.

Keeah smiled. "Something better. I want the wand to do nothing at all."

Magdy frowned. "Nothing? Not even —"

"No," said Keeah.

"But what about —"

"No," said Keeah.

"What sort of magic is that?" asked Hagdy.

"The only kind that Anga can handle," said Keeah. "None at all."

"How about some baby dragons?" said Magdy, popping open a small bottle and sniffing. "They'd be very cute —"

"Skip the dragons," said Keeah. "And please hurry. We'll need the wand very soon as part of my plan."

"Oh! You have a *plan*!" said Hagdy.

Keeah frowned. "It's getting there. Bring the wand to the Patio of Terror as soon as you're finished. I have other things to do."

"Ooh, sister, I feel young again," said Hagdy, clearing the workbench.

"And I feel even younger!" added Magdy.

Smiling to herself, Keeah rushed back down to the base of the cliffs. There she found Julie and Neal waiting for her. "Good, you're safe!"

"All thanks to me," said Neal. "I did my genie thing and we totally escaped."

"I told Pinch to let you go," said Keeah.

"See? I told you," said Julie. "There was no reason to sing your Zabilac song again."

Neal grumbled. "The important thing is we're together again. Phase One is complete."

"Freeing you was Phase Two," said Keeah.

"You've been busy," said Julie. "When do we get that wand?"

"Phase Five. Or maybe Seven," said Keeah, suddenly wondering how many phases her plan actually had. "Now, follow me. We haven't a moment to lose."

The three friends rushed around to the front of Anga's palace, where they spied Pinch talking intently with Anga. When the weasel king smiled, the sun broke through the trees.

"Phase Four," Keeah whispered. "Pinch is telling Anga who the knights are —"

"Who are they?" asked Julie.

Before Keeah could answer, they heard the creaking of wood and the splashing of water.

"Holy cow! I think that's the Skorth!" cried Neal. "This is even worse than the Patio of Terror!"

"No, no, this is a good thing," said Keeah.

Neal gulped. "If *this* is good, what's bad?"

"You mean besides your song?" said Julie.

Keeah spotted the patio entrance.

"When the Skorth demand the wand, Anga will get upset."

"Upset?" said Julie. "Yeah, a little."

Keeah nodded. "That's what I'm counting on. He'll get upset. Then they'll get upset. Then Anga will start a storm. Then the Skorth will attack. In all the craziness, we'll get the wand."

Neal counted on his fingers and frowned. "At which phase do we escape to safety?"

Keeah tried to smile. "I haven't gotten that far yet. Now, hush. We need to get to Anga's tower. Fly me up? Secretly?"

So Julie and Neal linked arms with Keeah and flew straight to the top of the throne tower. This time, they found a place for all three to hide — on a narrow balcony surrounding the throne room at the summit.

The throne room was a broad courtyard open to the sky and lit by lamps hung on bamboo posts. The lamps shed a golden light on Anga's leafy throne.

"I can see why Anga keeps this place to himself," said Neal. "It's pretty cool."

Pinch's troops were ranged on either side of the courtyard, while Anga stood in front of his throne, leaning first on one foot, then the other, holding the Ruby Wand high, then low, then forward, then at his waist. "Pinch, lower the cradle for our visitors!" he commanded.

As the cradle descended, Anga began to murmur to himself. "Skorth! My fearless knights . . . No, no, that's not right. Ahem . . . Skorth! Knights of valor . . . No, no. Ah, I have it! Warriors of the Skorth. My noble knights! Yes, that's it!"

"Anga wants to make a good impression on the Skorth," whispered Julie.

"I predict that's not going to happen," said Neal.

Suddenly, they heard grunting and the thrashing of leaves down below.

"They're coming," Keeah whispered, trying to remain calm. Her heart was pounding so quickly she thought it might explode.

*I hope this works!*

There came a sudden squeal from the dangling vines, and the cradle ascended.

"Finally!" said Anga. "My knights arrive!"

The courtyard darkened and cooled as three Skorth warriors stepped into the courtyard. The silver bones on the helmet of their leader gleamed in the golden lamplight. His bony feet clacked on the floor. He and his two companions wielded swords with blades as wavy as swift-moving water.

"I am Nok," said the Skorth leader.

"Ahem!" said Anga, rising from his throne. "Warriors of the Skorth — my noble knights — so long foretold —"

"Since Saturday," muttered Pinch.

"I am pleased to see you! To show allegiance to your new leader, please bow."

"Please . . . *what*?" growled the Skorth captain. "Did you say . . . *bow*?"

Pinch shot a worried look at Anga.

The weasel king cleared his throat, and a cloud moved overhead, darkening the courtyard for a moment before passing.

"If you would, yes," said Anga. "I like my underlings to bow. It makes me feel taller, you see."

"Anga's getting nervous," whispered Julie. "We should stop this."

"I think that's Phase Eight," said Keeah.

"We—shall—not—bow!" snarled Nok.

Anga's eyebrows twitched, and a second cloud appeared. It lingered, and the courtyard grew darker still.

"But perhaps you don't understand. I am King Anga," he said. "Possessor of the legendary Ruby Wand. The prophecy says I shall rule the Knights of the Ruby Wand. It's all in the prophecy. Pinch, *read* the prophecy!"

From his position next to the throne, Pinch shuddered. "Yes, Sire." He unrolled a sheet of yellow parchment. "The prophecy states that he who possesses the wand —"

"In other words, *me!*" said Anga.

"— shall rule the Knights of the Ruby Wand —"

"In other words, *you!*" said Anga.

The Skorth warriors looked at one another.

"So you see, it's very logical," said Anga. "And thus I repeat . . . please bow."

The three skeleton warriors raised their wavy swords high in the air.

"Oh, boy. Oh, boy," said Neal.

"Ditto," said Julie.

"We are not Knights of the Ruby Wand!" Nok snarled. "We are Warriors of the Skorth. We are allies of Lord Gethwing!"

*Splat!* A large drop of rain fell on the floor in front of Nok.

The sky thundered as Anga's silver tuft bristled. His fangs showed briefly. "*Lord* Gethwing? Well, he *can't* be very important, because *king* is better than *lord* any day. But just to be *sure*, I hereby pronounce myself *Emperor* Anga. So there!"

"This isn't going to be pretty," said Neal.

"I hereby pronounce you *dead*!" shouted the Skorth captain. "Men, charge the throne!"

With a clatter of bony feet, the Skorth leaped at the throne, their wavy swords flashing in the lamplight.

"Troops, protect your king!" yelled Pinch.

"Your *emperor*!" shouted Anga.

"Your *dead* emperor!" growled Nok.

"Phase Five!" cried Keeah. "Or Six!"

## Nine

## Mayhem!

"Traitors!" yelped Anga as he skittered on all fours toward the cradle. "*My* knights would never do this!"

"For the last time — we are *not* your knights!" said Nok. "Get the little weasel!"

One Skorth sliced the vines holding the cradle, sending it tumbling to the ground.

"Oh! Oh! Pinch, save me!" cried Anga.

"Run into the patio!" called Keeah, leaping down to the courtyard with Neal and Julie.

"Of Terror?" said Pinch.

"That's the one!" said Julie. "We'll defend you!"

The children rushed between the bony warriors and the weasels, tripping them up.

The warriors clattered to the courtyard floor, then jumped to their feet and charged the weasel again.

But as Anga's temper flared, and the little weasel grew afraid, icy winds roared across the tower, making it tremble. Lightning bolts flashed through the air like fiery arrows.

Keeah added to the mayhem by blasting at the Skorth, trying to hold them back. Undeterred, Nok and his companions kept up their attack, driving Anga and the kids down to the patio.

"Follow me!" said Neal, his turban low on his head. "I think I remember the way!"

*Whack-whack-whack!* The Skorth chopped away at the patio floors, walls, ladders, and stairs to get at Anga and the children.

"You're scaring me to death!" said Anga.

"Good!" said Nok. "You'll be dead like us!"

"You don't have to tell me," said Anga. "I see your backbone through your front bone!"

"Give us the wand!" shouted Nok.

"Not on your life!" said Anga.

"On yours, then!" snarled Nok.

With every moment, Anga grew angrier and more afraid. The sky churned with dense black clouds. Rain pummeled the palace. Hailstones the size of baseballs fell like a shower of bombs.

"This way to the ground — I think!" said Pinch, plowing his way to a lower level.

"When you escape, run to the cliffs," said Keeah. "Julie, Neal, turn and stand fast —"

Keeah took up position at the top of a set of stairs. Her fingers aimed a quick spray of violet sparks at the Skorth, sending them all clattering to the jungle floor below.

"Yes!" shouted Neal.

"Ha! You will not stop us!" said Nok. "That bug gave us orders to bring the wand to Gethwing, and bring it we shall!"

Neal grinned down at them. "Three deadies against a wizard, a genie, and a wingwolf girl? I don't think so —"

Nok scowled. "Then let's bring more players into the game. Indus, call the others!"

"No!" gasped Julie. "Stop him —"

Keeah sent a blast at the skeleton

warrior named Indus, but he twisted aside and produced a tiny horn from his belt and blew into it.

*Ooo-uuu-oooo!*

The long, low wail was answered a second later by a similar call from the distant shore.

*Ooo-uuu-oooo!*

"Oh, that can't be good," said Neal. "What phase is the one where all the Skorth come?"

"Six and a Half, I think?" said Keeah, sending a blast of sparks at the bony warriors, then dragging her friends down the stairs to the next level. The weasels were running in circles, still trying to find a way out.

"Anga, the Skorth are bringing their entire navy to attack your jungle empire!" said Keeah. "Because you have the wand. Look!"

The Skorth ships docked on the distant shore. Gangplanks were out in a flash and were soon filled with hundreds of sword-wielding warriors. Within moments, the sounds of hundreds of thumping bony feet filled the jungle.

"They're coming!" said Julie.

"Give us the wand!" Nok shouted from the jungle below, slashing his blade wildly in the air. "Or we'll tear down your palace — and your jungle — tree by tree!"

Anga suddenly slumped to the floor.

"What is it, Sire?" asked Pinch.

The weasel leader shuddered from tail to snout. The fringes on his shoulders quivered. The tuft on his head wilted. "I can't. I love my sunny jungle. I don't want it destroyed. It can't be ruined. I don't *want* this anymore!"

With that, he tossed the Ruby Wand to Keeah.

Neal blinked in surprise. "That was easy."

"Too easy," said Julie. "Keeah, the Skorth are coming fast. Make more storms. Big ones. Stop them!"

Keeah felt the power of the Ruby Wand running through her veins and knew in an instant the strong magic that Galen could control with it. But she knew that getting angry solved nothing. It often made things worse. She found she wanted all the anger to end.

And without anger, there was no storm.

"Sorry, guys. I can't . . . ," she said.

So the storm disappeared. The sun peeped through the leaves. The wind vanished into a soft, warm breeze.

"Here they come!" said Pinch.

In a flash, there they were, thousands

of skeleton warriors, hacking down the trees with their wavy blades.

"They dare not attack us here," said Anga.

"They dare," said Julie. "The Skorth are bad that way."

"We will destroy you!" shouted Nok. "Forward, my men — come to us!"

The jungle floor teemed with fearsome Skorth warriors. Within minutes, they had surrounded Anga's palace.

"Now!" bellowed the Skorth leader.

The bony warriors began chopping at the palace walls. And the tower began to tip.

# Ten

# What Happened with the Wand

With no wind or rain or lightning to stop them, the Skorth hacked viciously at the tower. It teetered from side to side.

"There are hundreds of them," said Julie.

"Thousands!" said Neal.

"Lots!" agreed Pinch. "And they aren't nice!"

Keeah knew what she had to do.

"Anga, there's . . . something in my sandal. Could you hold the wand for a second?"

"Certainly, dear," said the weasel king, taking up the wand again.

"What are you doing?" whispered Pinch.

"Adding a new phase," Keeah whispered back.

*Hack-hack-hack!* The Skorth slashed at the palace. Chunks of it fell to the ground.

"That — makes — me — so — angry!" boomed Anga.

His ears shot straight up like iron plates. The tuft of silver fur coiled into wiry, fire-tipped spikes.

Lightning flashed from the wand.

"His anger *is* the storm!" said Julie.

"Except that it's not just a storm anymore," said Neal. "Look. . . ."

A funnel, darker than the darkening sky, as dark as night itself, swirled across the sky. It was heading straight for the jungle. It was growing bigger and wider as it tore toward them.

"A hurricane!" cried Pinch.

As Anga's face grew more menacing, the storm broadened over the whole of Doobesh. It flailed at the sea as if trying to turn it upside down. Rain and wind slashed at the ships.

"Give us the wand!" Nok demanded.

"You shall not have it!" Anga boomed, his voice as thunderous as the storm itself.

The distant wail of a Skorth horn pierced the storm's increasing howl. This time it wasn't a battle call. It was a distress call.

"The storm is sinking our navy!" growled Nok. "Forget the wand! Save our fleet!"

"Back — where — you — came — from!" cried Anga. "All the way back!" Thrusting the wand at the warriors, he produced a wind as strong as an iron wall. It thundered at the Skorth, hurling them head over bony heels all the way out of the jungle to the shore.

The skeleton warriors barely made it back up the gangplanks before Anga's hurricane blew the entire navy — twenty ragged ghost ships — helter-skelter back toward the Horns of Ko.

One ship after another was dashed against the giant stones and onto the sharp cliffs. Planks shattered. Masts fell. Ferocious winds ripped the ships' ragged sails to nothing.

The shrieks and wails of the Skorth sailors could be heard all the way back at Anga's throne tower. The storm kept on until the great smashing stones closed behind the ships, sealing them from the Sea of Droon.

"Behold the wrath of Anga!" boomed the weasel leader.

"Yahoo!" shouted Neal. "Your trick worked, Keeah!"

Anga whirled around. "Trick? What trick? I don't like tricks —"

"Now you've done it," said Pinch, shaking his head.

Anga growled fiercely, and the storm tore right back through the jungle. It stopped right over the tower.

Lightning blasted at them, and the tower began to fall apart.

"It's out of control!" said Neal.

***Take — the — wand!*** Keeah said silently.

In a flash, the three kids — and Pinch — leaped on Anga. Together they wrestled him all the way to the ground below the tower, where, with one powerful move, Keeah clamped her hands on the Ruby Wand.

"But — it's — mine!" Anga wailed.

"Sisters — now!" yelled Keeah.

*BLONG-G-G-G!*

A flash of blinding light exploded and Anga was heaved to the ground. "Owww!"

The witches Hagdy and Magdy stood right over the weasel king. In his hands was what appeared to be the Ruby Wand. But Keeah knew it was not.

She knew it was not, because at that very moment, she held the real wand behind her back.

As Anga waved the new wand, the clouds vanished into a bright blue sky, the sun blazed down, and the storm was no more than a memory. The Sea of Droon

was as calm and bright and smooth as a sheet of glass.

Anga smiled. "Well! I suppose I really *am* the most powerful tree weasel in all of Droon. Not only have I defeated the mighty Skorth, but I can finally control the weather!"

Laughing, he waved the wand at the sunny sky above. "I'm quite the best!"

"Yes," said Pinch. "Yes, you are." Then he leaned over to Keeah. "He may not even notice. At least, not at first. But we thank you."

Keeah and her friends looked at the black and choppy waves of the Serpent Sea and saw the Skorth navy limping back to the horizon.

Pinch turned to the kids. "So I guess you're actually them, aren't you?"

"Them who?" asked Neal.

"The Knights of the Ruby Wand," said the weasel. "Which is fine. Me and my men don't want to be. Never did."

"I don't think I'll really be needing you," Anga told the children. "Not with all my newfound power. This calls for an official ceremony. Bow. Please."

This time, the children bowed happily as Anga tapped their shoulders with his wand.

"I dub thee Knights of the Ruby Wand!"

Suddenly — *pop-pop-pop!* — three baby dragons appeared next to the children.

"We couldn't resist," said Magdy. "I guess we still do have a little magic left."

"And because I'm older, I have a little more!" said Hagdy.

The baby dragons squealed in unison, then flew off into the jungle.

A blue flare exploded overhead, and a

sudden bright laugh echoed down from the top of the cliffs. On the deck of the wind-wagon, Max, Hob, Batamogi, and Khan were leaping up and down.

"We've done it!" Max called down to Keeah, Julie, and Neal. "We've got Eric's cure!"

Keeah's heart beat faster. They were closer than ever to helping Eric. She smiled, remembering the strange way he had helped *her* today.

She turned to her friends. "We've won this time. But we can't rest. There are now only three days left before Gethwing attacks Jaffa City. We need Eric here with us."

"And Galen," said Julie. "Let's do what we need to do."

"It's the perfect time for Phase Nine," said Neal.

"There is no Phase Nine," said Keeah.

"There is now," said Neal. "It's called The Singing of the Theme Song!"

And before his friends could stop him, Neal launched into his song. As before, the first verse was all about him. But the second was all about his friends.

*"Through thick and thin they go,*
*And battle every foe*
*From Plud to Silversnow.*
*They're best of friends . . . ho . . . ho!"*

Julie laughed. "Getting better, Neal, but don't stop working on it."

"Are you kidding?" he said. "This is just the tip of the iceberg —"

"Please, no," murmured Pinch.

And so, after saying good-bye to the tree weasels, Neal and his friends sang all the way up the cliff to the windwagon and to their next adventure.